MARVEL

AVENGERS ULTRON REVOLUTION

DEHULKED #4

ABDO
Spotlight

ABDOBOOKS.COM

Reinforced library bound edition published in 2020 by Spotlight,
a division of ABDO, PO Box 398166, Minneapolis, Minnesota 55439.
Spotlight produces high-quality reinforced library bound editions for
schools and libraries. Published by agreement with Marvel Characters, Inc.

Printed in the United States of America, North Mankato, Minnesota.
042019
092019

THIS BOOK CONTAINS
RECYCLED MATERIALS

marvelkids.com
© 2020 MARVEL

Library of Congress Control Number: 2018965956

Publisher's Cataloging-in-Publication Data

Names: Caramagna, Joe; Giacoppo, Paul, authors. | Marvel Animation Studios,
    illustrator.
Title: Dehulked / by Joe Caramagna ; Paul Giacoppo; illustrated by Marvel
    Animation Studios.
Description: Minneapolis, Minnesota : Spotlight, 2020. | Series: Avengers: ultron
    revolution; #4
Summary: When his old lab assistant Igor Drenkov takes Hulk's powers away with a
    gamma energy-stealing weapon, Bruce has to show the Avengers he's still part
    of the team as they work to get his powers back.
Identifiers: ISBN 9781532143496 (lib. bdg.)
Subjects: LCSH: Avengers (Fictitious characters)--Juvenile fiction. | Superheroes--
    Juvenile fiction. | Superpowers--Juvenile fiction. | Gamma rays--Juvenile fiction.
    | Graphic novels--Juvenile fiction. | Incredible Hulk (Fictitious character)--
    Juvenile fiction. | Science--Experiments--Juvenile fiction. | Comic books, strips,
    etc--Juvenile fiction.
Classification: DDC 741.5--dc23

Spotlight

A Division of ABDO
abdobooks.com

Dr. Bruce Banner was a brilliant scientist who attempted to create a weapon so powerful it would deter future wars: the gamma bomb! After being caught in the blast of an ill-fated bomb test, his life was changed forever.

Whenever angered or threatened, Dr. Banner now transforms into an incredible engine of destruction, a green behemoth known as THE HULK!

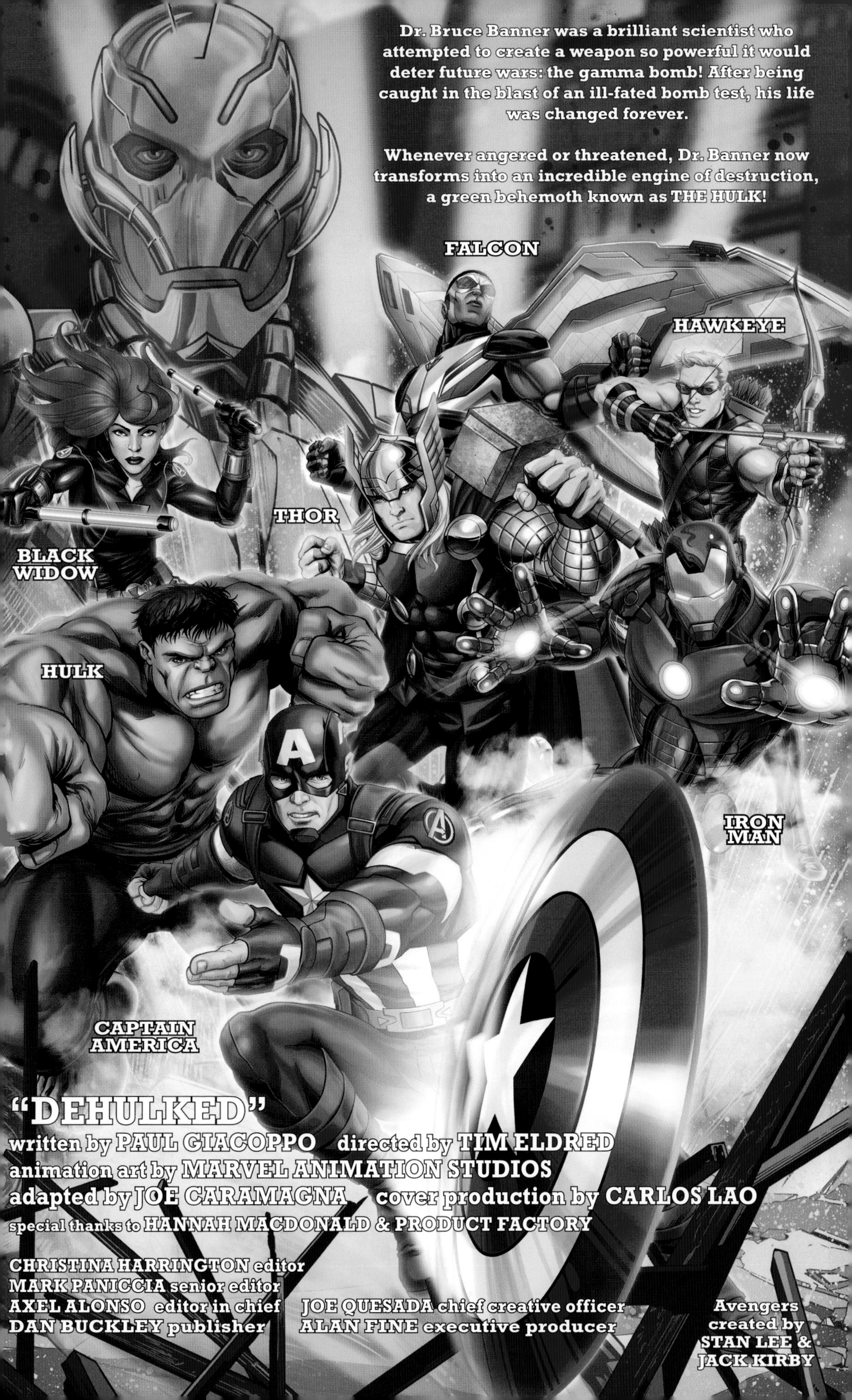
FALCON
HAWKEYE
THOR
BLACK WIDOW
HULK
IRON MAN
CAPTAIN AMERICA

"DEHULKED"

written by PAUL GIACOPPO directed by TIM ELDRED
animation art by MARVEL ANIMATION STUDIOS
adapted by JOE CARAMAGNA cover production by CARLOS LAO
special thanks to HANNAH MACDONALD & PRODUCT FACTORY

CHRISTINA HARRINGTON editor
MARK PANICCIA senior editor
AXEL ALONSO editor in chief
DAN BUCKLEY publisher
JOE QUESADA chief creative officer
ALAN FINE executive producer

Avengers created by STAN LEE & JACK KIRBY

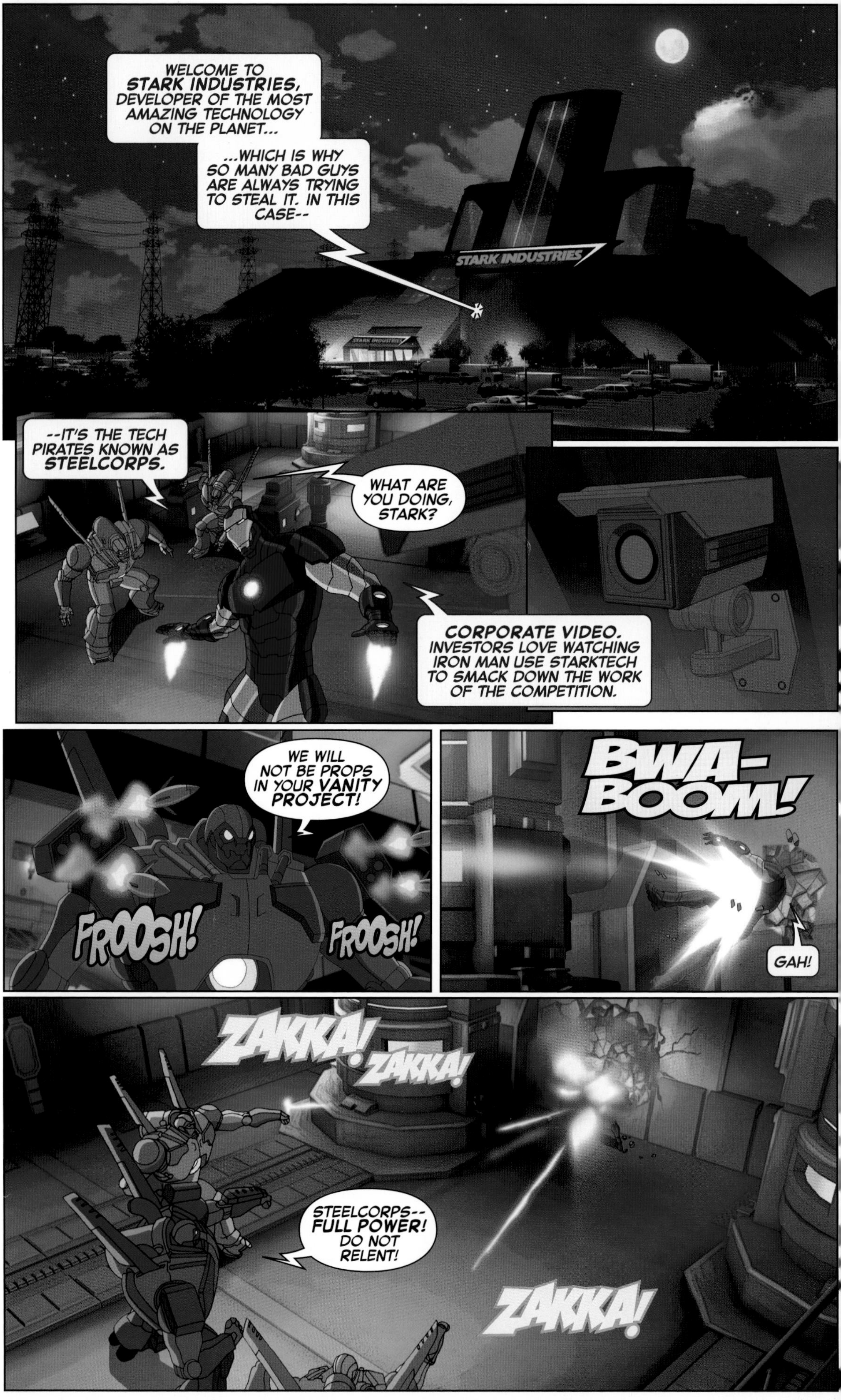

WELCOME TO STARK INDUSTRIES, DEVELOPER OF THE MOST AMAZING TECHNOLOGY ON THE PLANET...
...WHICH IS WHY SO MANY BAD GUYS ARE ALWAYS TRYING TO STEAL IT. IN THIS CASE--
STARK INDUSTRIES
--IT'S THE TECH PIRATES KNOWN AS STEELCORPS.
WHAT ARE YOU DOING, STARK?
CORPORATE VIDEO. INVESTORS LOVE WATCHING IRON MAN USE STARKTECH TO SMACK DOWN THE WORK OF THE COMPETITION.
WE WILL NOT BE PROPS IN YOUR VANITY PROJECT!
FROOSH!
FROOSH!
BWA-BOOM!
GAH!
ZAKKA!
ZAKKA!
STEELCORPS--FULL POWER! DO NOT RELENT!
ZAKKA!

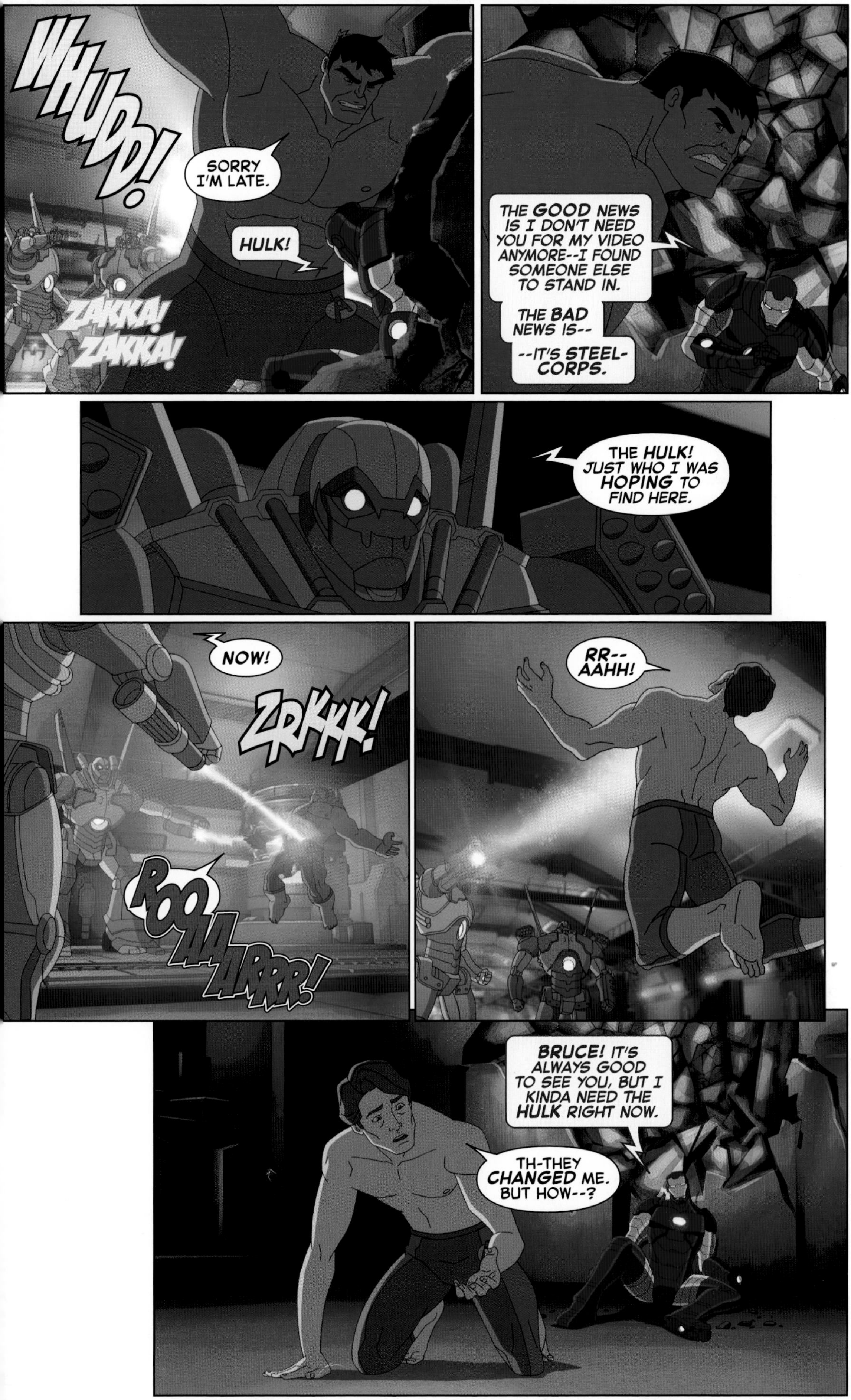
WHUDD!
SORRY I'M LATE.
HULK!
ZAKKA! ZAKKA!
THE GOOD NEWS IS I DON'T NEED YOU FOR MY VIDEO ANYMORE--I FOUND SOMEONE ELSE TO STAND IN.
THE BAD NEWS IS--
--IT'S STEEL-CORPS.
THE HULK! JUST WHO I WAS HOPING TO FIND HERE.
NOW!
ZRKKK!
ROOAAARRR!
RR--AAHH!
BRUCE! IT'S ALWAYS GOOD TO SEE YOU, BUT I KINDA NEED THE HULK RIGHT NOW.
TH-THEY CHANGED ME. BUT HOW--?

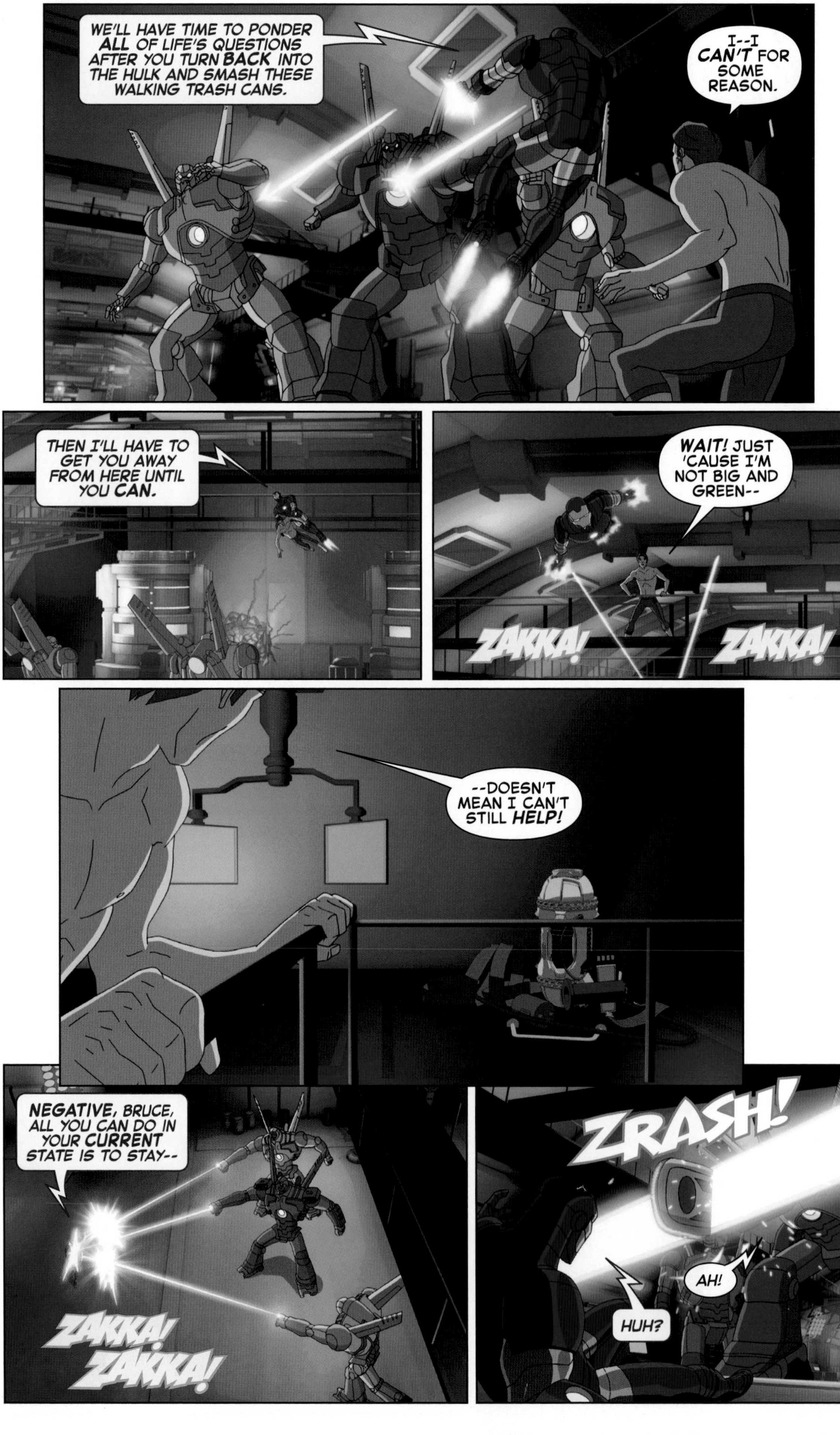
WE'LL HAVE TIME TO PONDER ALL OF LIFE'S QUESTIONS AFTER YOU TURN BACK INTO THE HULK AND SMASH THESE WALKING TRASH CANS.
I--I CAN'T FOR SOME REASON.
THEN I'LL HAVE TO GET YOU AWAY FROM HERE UNTIL YOU CAN.
WAIT! JUST 'CAUSE I'M NOT BIG AND GREEN--
ZAKKA!
ZAKKA!
--DOESN'T MEAN I CAN'T STILL HELP!
NEGATIVE, BRUCE, ALL YOU CAN DO IN YOUR CURRENT STATE IS TO STAY--
ZAKKA! ZAKKA!
ZRASH!
AH!
HUH?

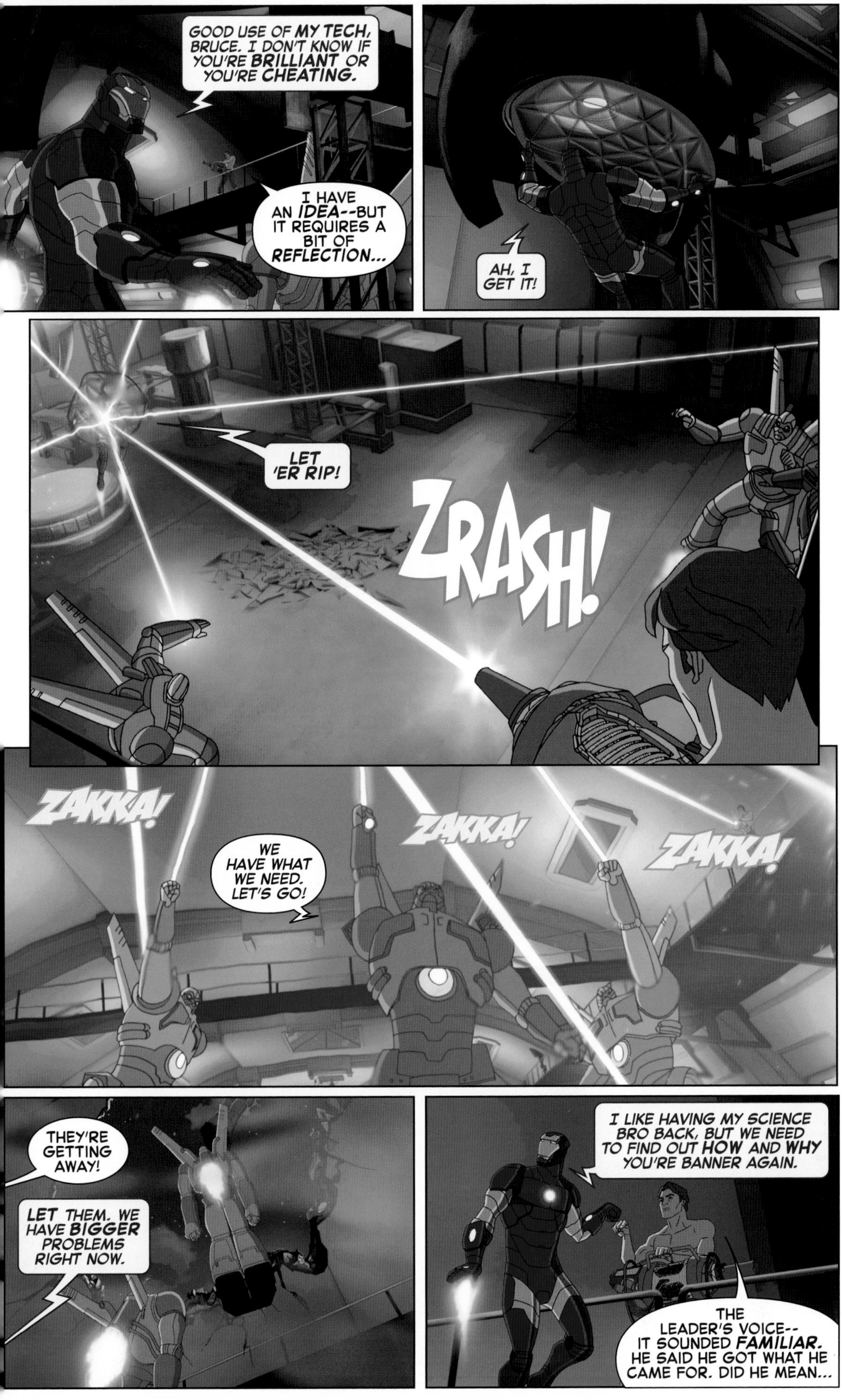
GOOD USE OF MY TECH, BRUCE. I DON'T KNOW IF YOU'RE BRILLIANT OR YOU'RE CHEATING.
I HAVE AN IDEA--BUT IT REQUIRES A BIT OF REFLECTION...
AH, I GET IT!
LET 'ER RIP!
ZRASH!
ZAKKA!
ZAKKA!
ZAKKA!
WE HAVE WHAT WE NEED. LET'S GO!
THEY'RE GETTING AWAY!
LET THEM. WE HAVE BIGGER PROBLEMS RIGHT NOW.
I LIKE HAVING MY SCIENCE BRO BACK, BUT WE NEED TO FIND OUT HOW AND WHY YOU'RE BANNER AGAIN.
THE LEADER'S VOICE-- IT SOUNDED FAMILIAR. HE SAID HE GOT WHAT HE CAME FOR. DID HE MEAN...

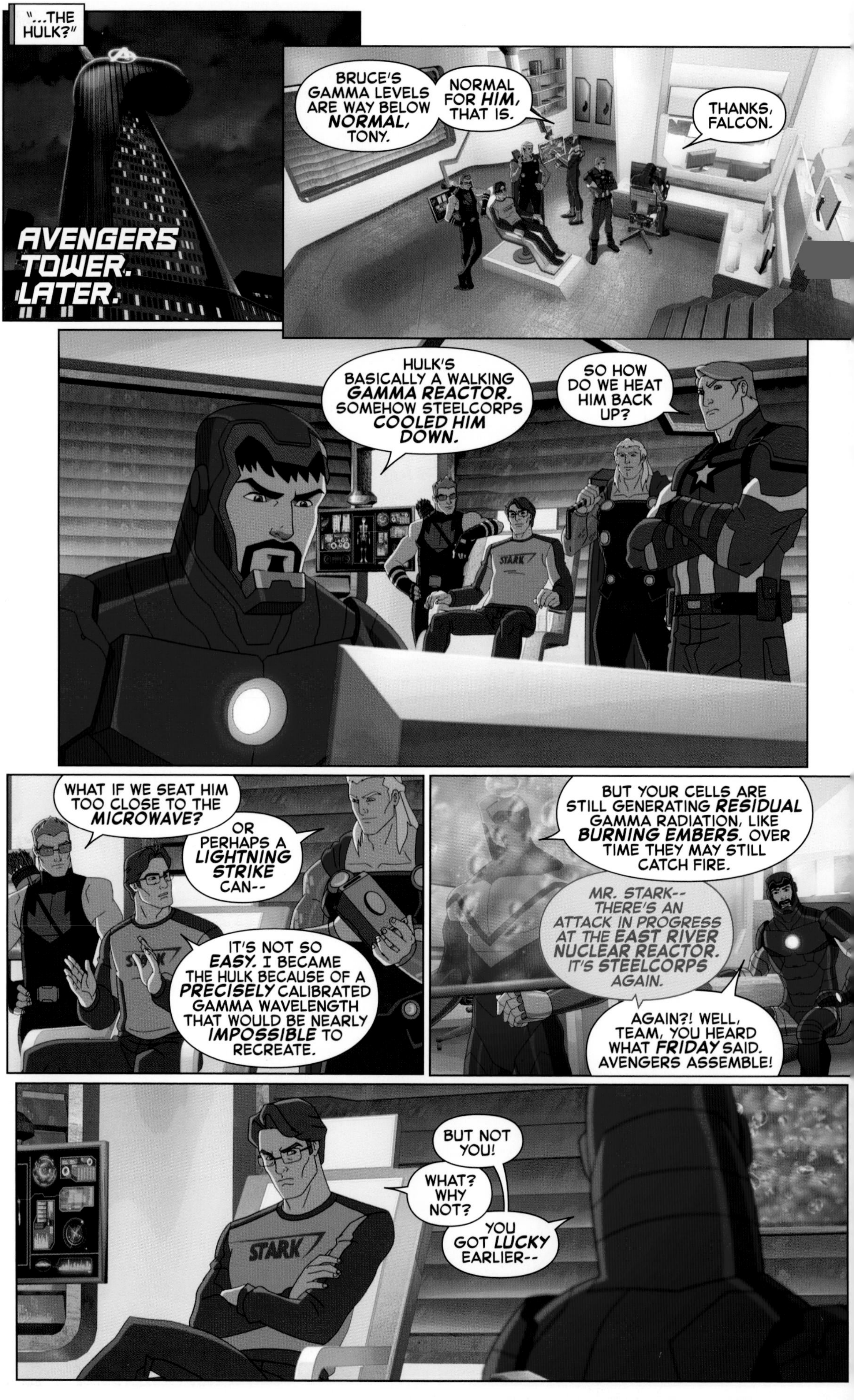
"...THE HULK?"
AVENGERS TOWER. LATER.
BRUCE'S GAMMA LEVELS ARE WAY BELOW NORMAL, TONY.
NORMAL FOR HIM, THAT IS.
THANKS, FALCON.
HULK'S BASICALLY A WALKING GAMMA REACTOR. SOMEHOW STEELCORPS COOLED HIM DOWN.
SO HOW DO WE HEAT HIM BACK UP?
STARK
WHAT IF WE SEAT HIM TOO CLOSE TO THE MICROWAVE?
OR PERHAPS A LIGHTNING STRIKE CAN--
IT'S NOT SO EASY. I BECAME THE HULK BECAUSE OF A PRECISELY CALIBRATED GAMMA WAVELENGTH THAT WOULD BE NEARLY IMPOSSIBLE TO RECREATE.
BUT YOUR CELLS ARE STILL GENERATING RESIDUAL GAMMA RADIATION, LIKE BURNING EMBERS. OVER TIME THEY MAY STILL CATCH FIRE.
MR. STARK-- THERE'S AN ATTACK IN PROGRESS AT THE EAST RIVER NUCLEAR REACTOR. IT'S STEELCORPS AGAIN.
AGAIN?! WELL, TEAM, YOU HEARD WHAT FRIDAY SAID. AVENGERS ASSEMBLE!
BUT NOT YOU!
WHAT? WHY NOT?
YOU GOT LUCKY EARLIER--
STARK

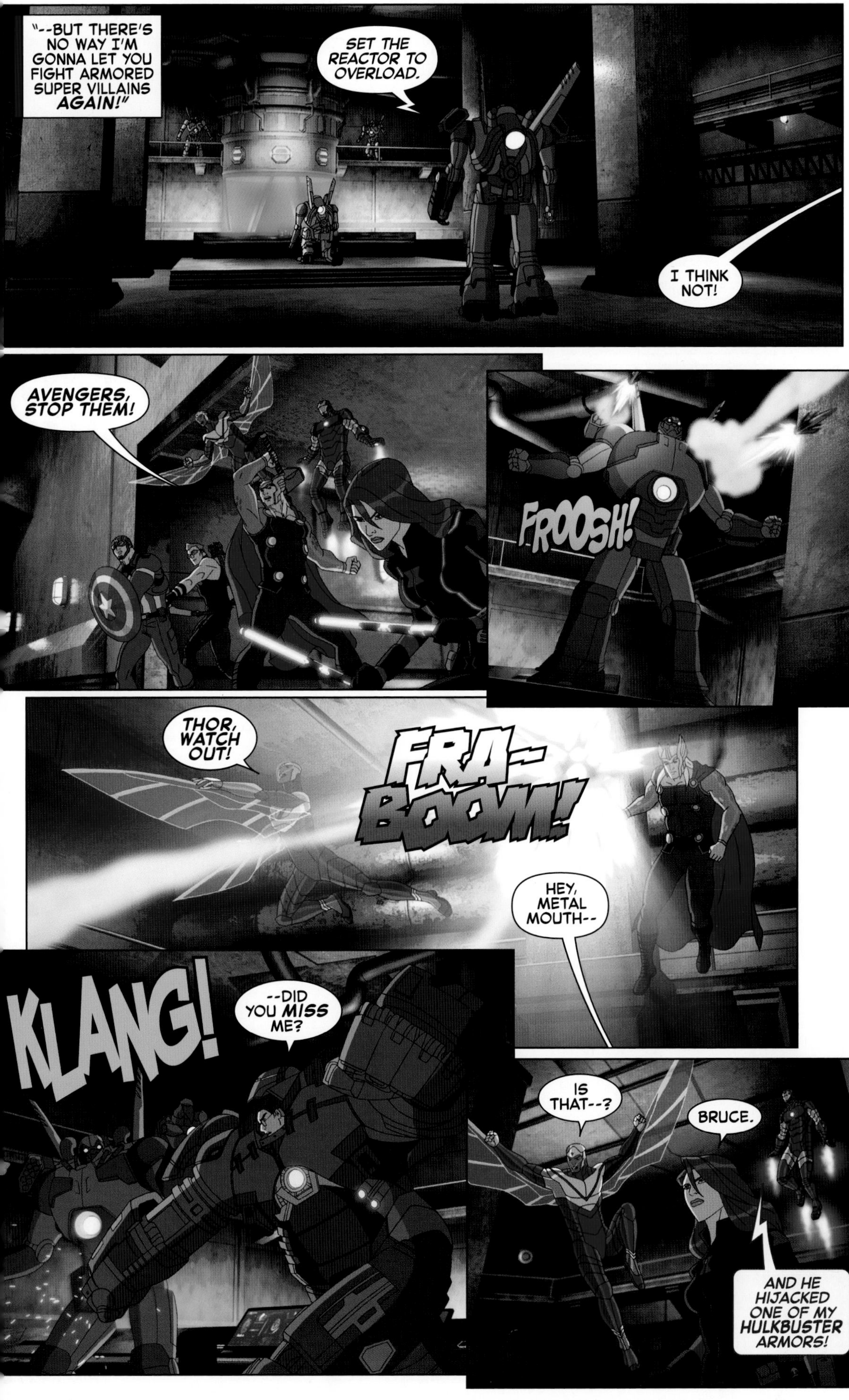
"--BUT THERE'S NO WAY I'M GONNA LET YOU FIGHT ARMORED SUPER VILLAINS AGAIN!"
SET THE REACTOR TO OVERLOAD.
I THINK NOT!
AVENGERS, STOP THEM!
FROOSH!
THOR, WATCH OUT!
FRA-BOOM!
HEY, METAL MOUTH--
KLANG!
--DID YOU MISS ME?
IS THAT--?
BRUCE.
AND HE HIJACKED ONE OF MY HULKBUSTER ARMORS!

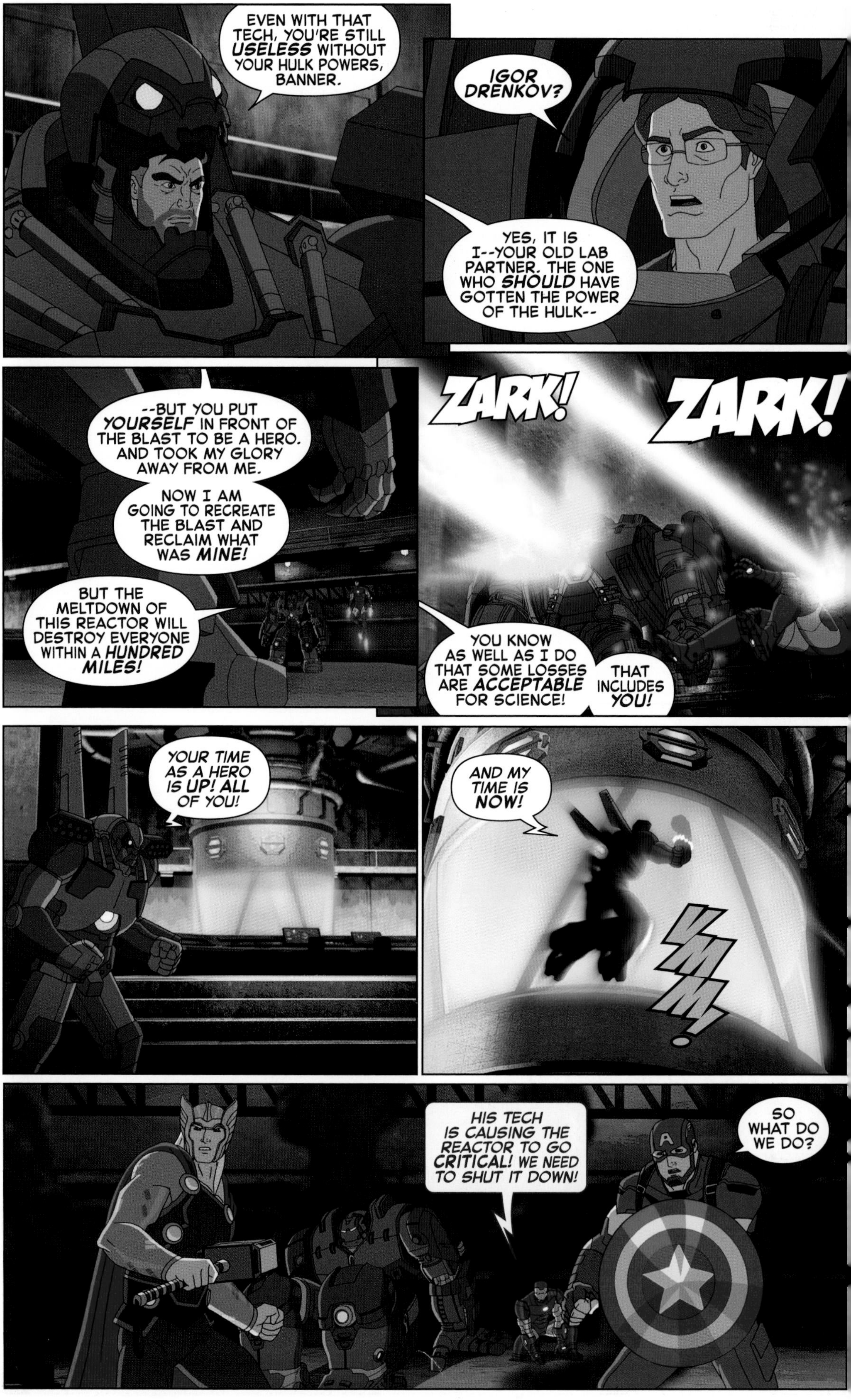
EVEN WITH THAT TECH, YOU'RE STILL USELESS WITHOUT YOUR HULK POWERS, BANNER.
IGOR DRENKOV?
YES, IT IS I--YOUR OLD LAB PARTNER. THE ONE WHO SHOULD HAVE GOTTEN THE POWER OF THE HULK--
--BUT YOU PUT YOURSELF IN FRONT OF THE BLAST TO BE A HERO. AND TOOK MY GLORY AWAY FROM ME.
NOW I AM GOING TO RECREATE THE BLAST AND RECLAIM WHAT WAS MINE!
BUT THE MELTDOWN OF THIS REACTOR WILL DESTROY EVERYONE WITHIN A HUNDRED MILES!
ZARK!
ZARK!
YOU KNOW AS WELL AS I DO THAT SOME LOSSES ARE ACCEPTABLE FOR SCIENCE!
THAT INCLUDES YOU!
YOUR TIME AS A HERO IS UP! ALL OF YOU!
AND MY TIME IS NOW!
VMM!
HIS TECH IS CAUSING THE REACTOR TO GO CRITICAL! WE NEED TO SHUT IT DOWN!
SO WHAT DO WE DO?

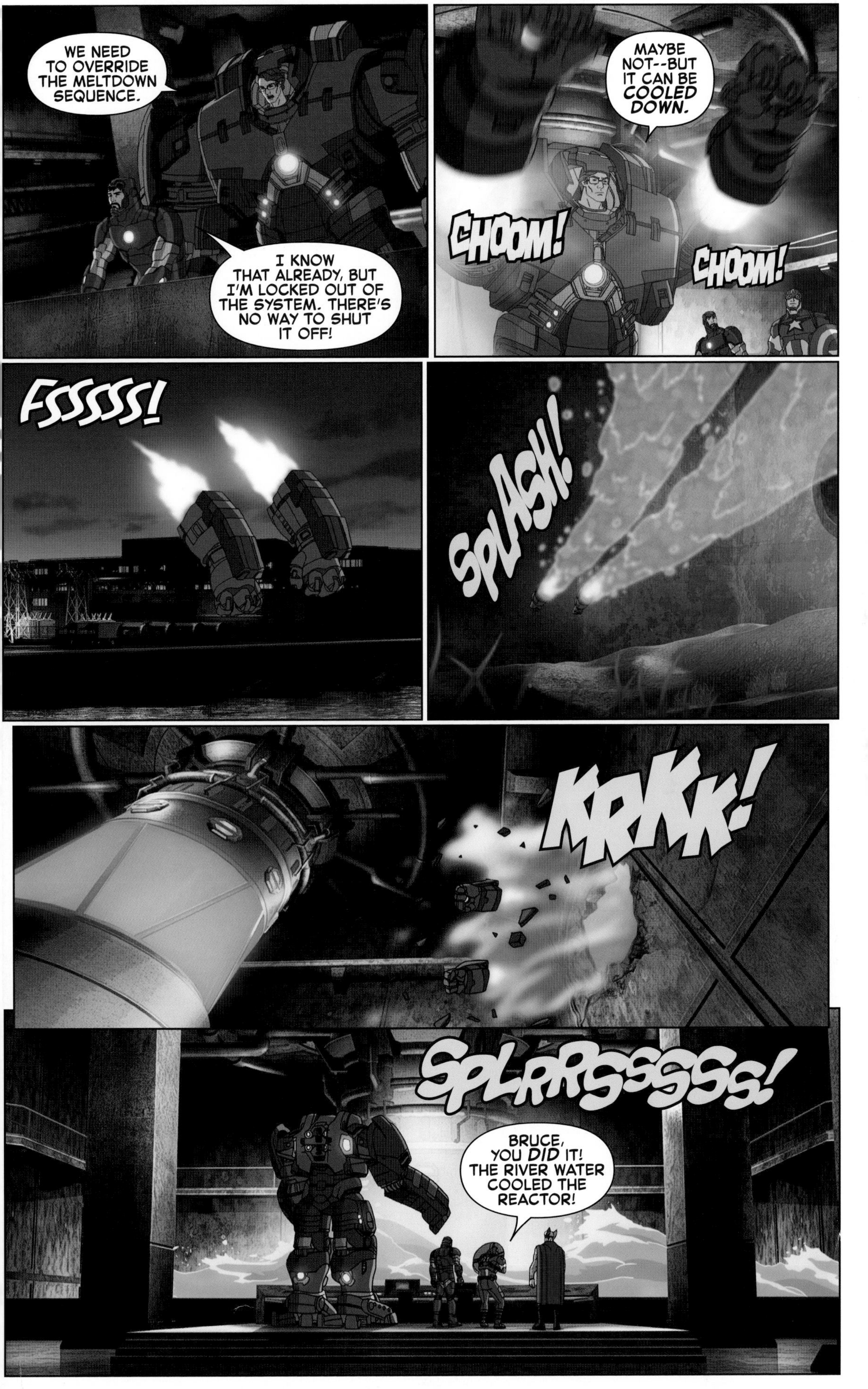
WE NEED TO OVERRIDE THE MELTDOWN SEQUENCE.
I KNOW THAT ALREADY, BUT I'M LOCKED OUT OF THE SYSTEM. THERE'S NO WAY TO SHUT IT OFF!
MAYBE NOT--BUT IT CAN BE COOLED DOWN.
CHOOM!
CHOOM!
FSSSSS!
SPLASH!
KRKK!
SPLRRSSSSSS!
BRUCE, YOU DID IT! THE RIVER WATER COOLED THE REACTOR!

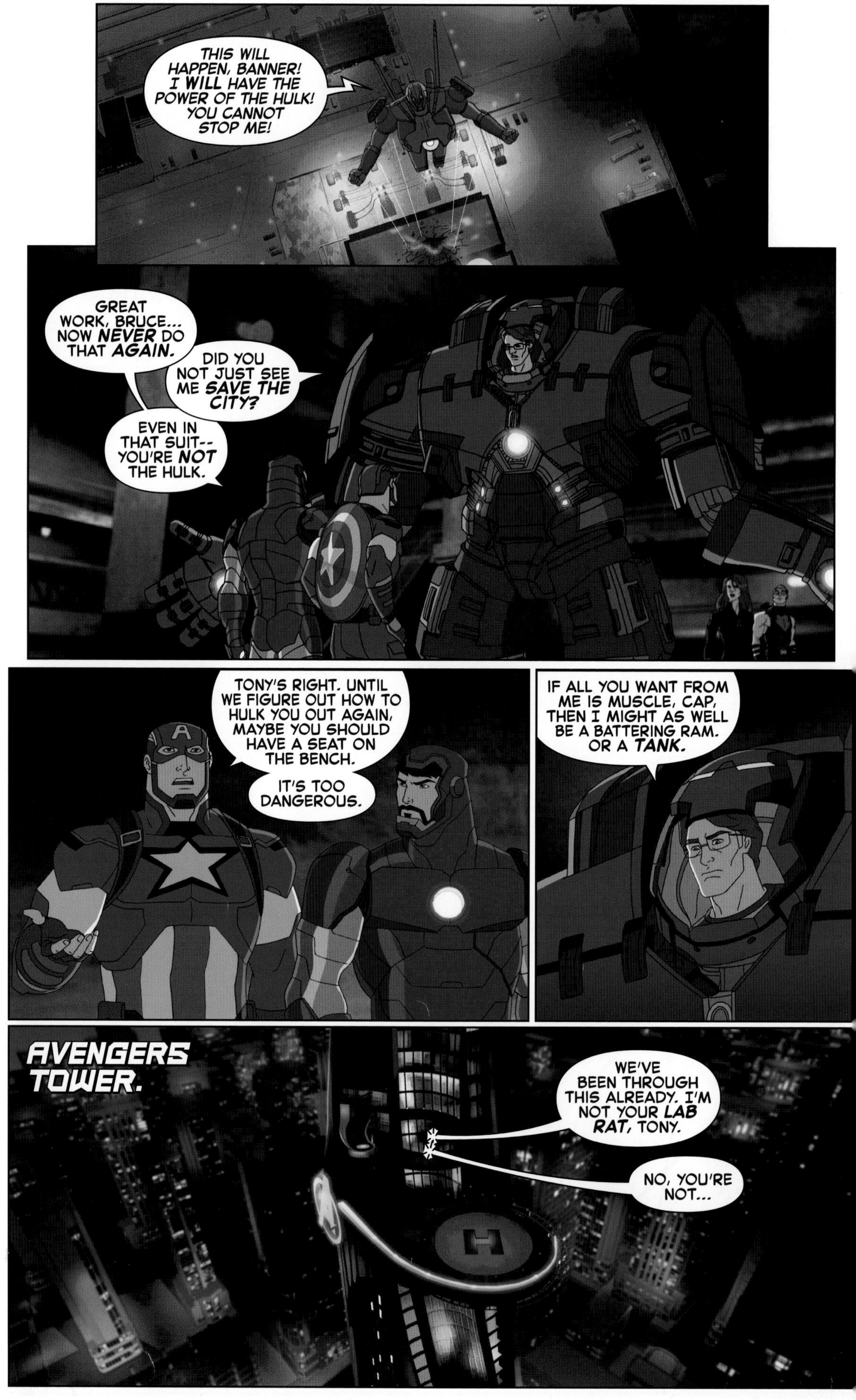
THIS WILL HAPPEN, BANNER! I WILL HAVE THE POWER OF THE HULK! YOU CANNOT STOP ME!
GREAT WORK, BRUCE... NOW NEVER DO THAT AGAIN.
DID YOU NOT JUST SEE ME SAVE THE CITY?
EVEN IN THAT SUIT--YOU'RE NOT THE HULK.
TONY'S RIGHT. UNTIL WE FIGURE OUT HOW TO HULK YOU OUT AGAIN, MAYBE YOU SHOULD HAVE A SEAT ON THE BENCH.
IT'S TOO DANGEROUS.
IF ALL YOU WANT FROM ME IS MUSCLE, CAP, THEN I MIGHT AS WELL BE A BATTERING RAM. OR A TANK.
AVENGERS TOWER.
WE'VE BEEN THROUGH THIS ALREADY. I'M NOT YOUR LAB RAT, TONY.
NO, YOU'RE NOT...

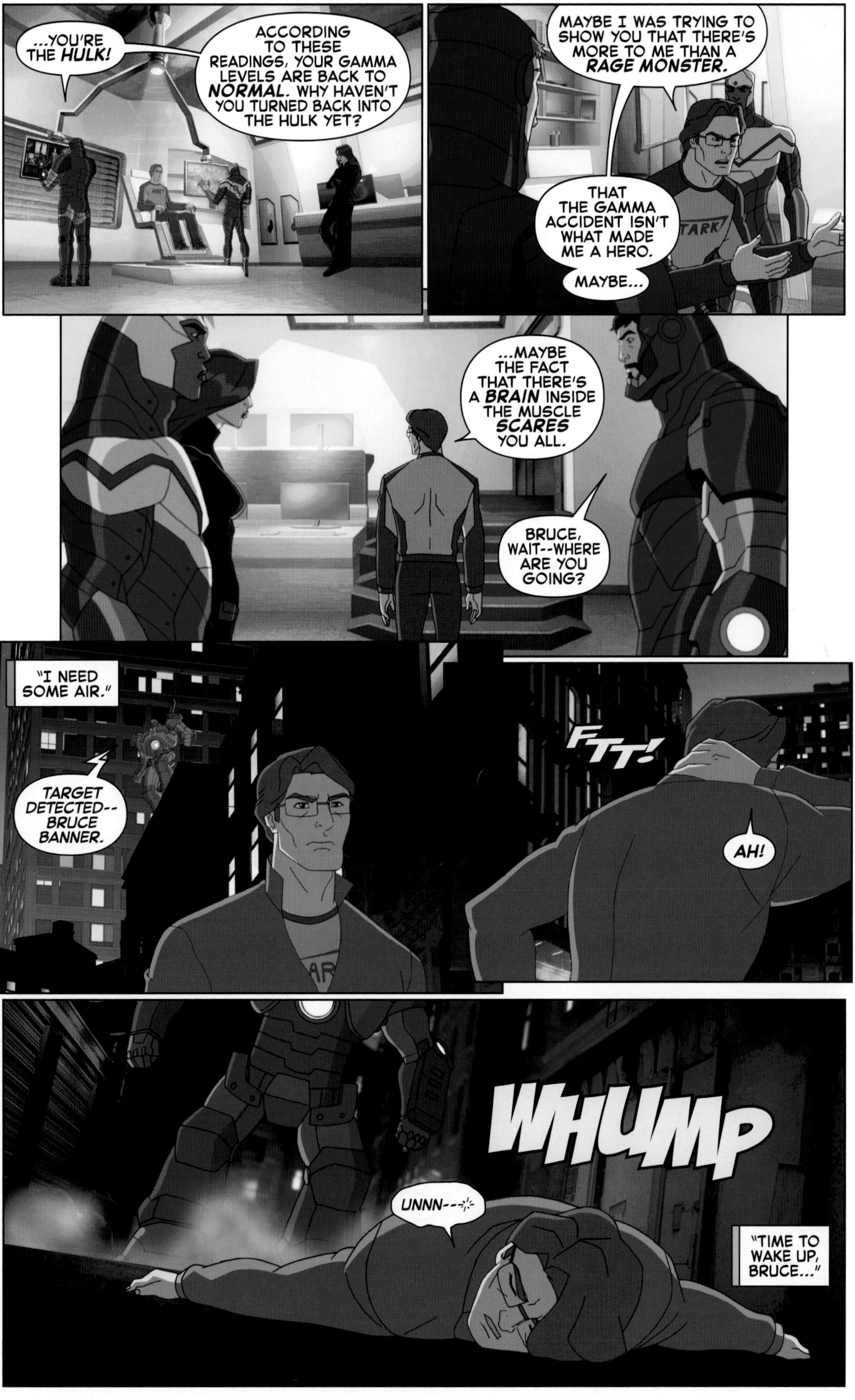
...YOU'RE THE HULK!
ACCORDING TO THESE READINGS, YOUR GAMMA LEVELS ARE BACK TO NORMAL. WHY HAVEN'T YOU TURNED BACK INTO THE HULK YET?
MAYBE I WAS TRYING TO SHOW YOU THAT THERE'S MORE TO ME THAN A RAGE MONSTER.
THAT THE GAMMA ACCIDENT ISN'T WHAT MADE ME A HERO.
MAYBE...
...MAYBE THE FACT THAT THERE'S A BRAIN INSIDE THE MUSCLE SCARES YOU ALL.
BRUCE, WAIT--WHERE ARE YOU GOING?
"I NEED SOME AIR."
TARGET DETECTED--BRUCE BANNER.
FTT!
AH!
WHUMP
UNNN--
"TIME TO WAKE UP, BRUCE..."

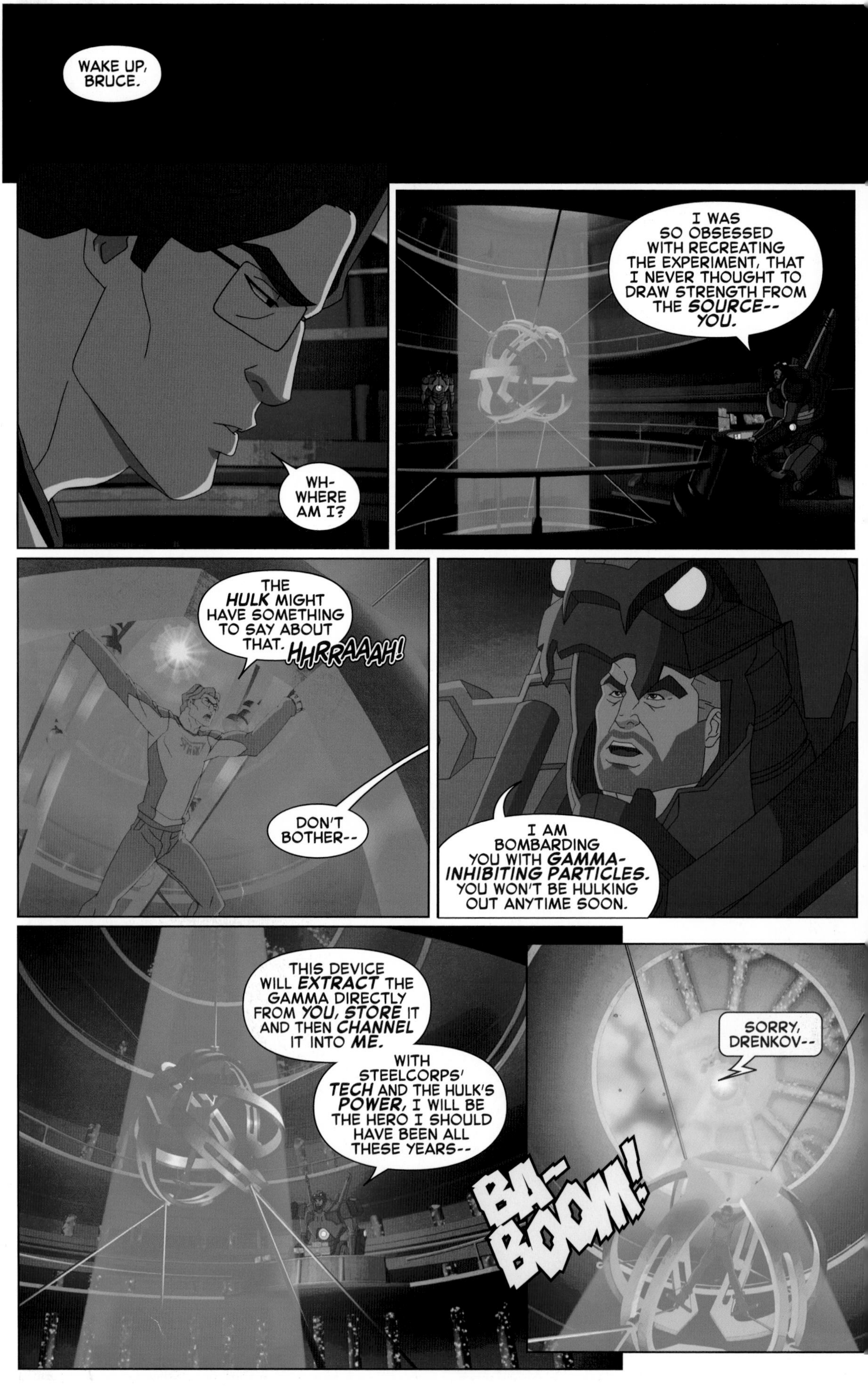
WAKE UP, BRUCE.
WH- WHERE AM I?
I WAS SO OBSESSED WITH RECREATING THE EXPERIMENT, THAT I NEVER THOUGHT TO DRAW STRENGTH FROM THE SOURCE-- YOU.
THE HULK MIGHT HAVE SOMETHING TO SAY ABOUT THAT. HHRRAAAH!
DON'T BOTHER--
I AM BOMBARDING YOU WITH GAMMA-INHIBITING PARTICLES. YOU WON'T BE HULKING OUT ANYTIME SOON.
THIS DEVICE WILL EXTRACT THE GAMMA DIRECTLY FROM YOU, STORE IT AND THEN CHANNEL IT INTO ME.
WITH STEELCORPS' TECH AND THE HULK'S POWER, I WILL BE THE HERO I SHOULD HAVE BEEN ALL THESE YEARS--
SORRY, DRENKOV--
BA-BOOM!

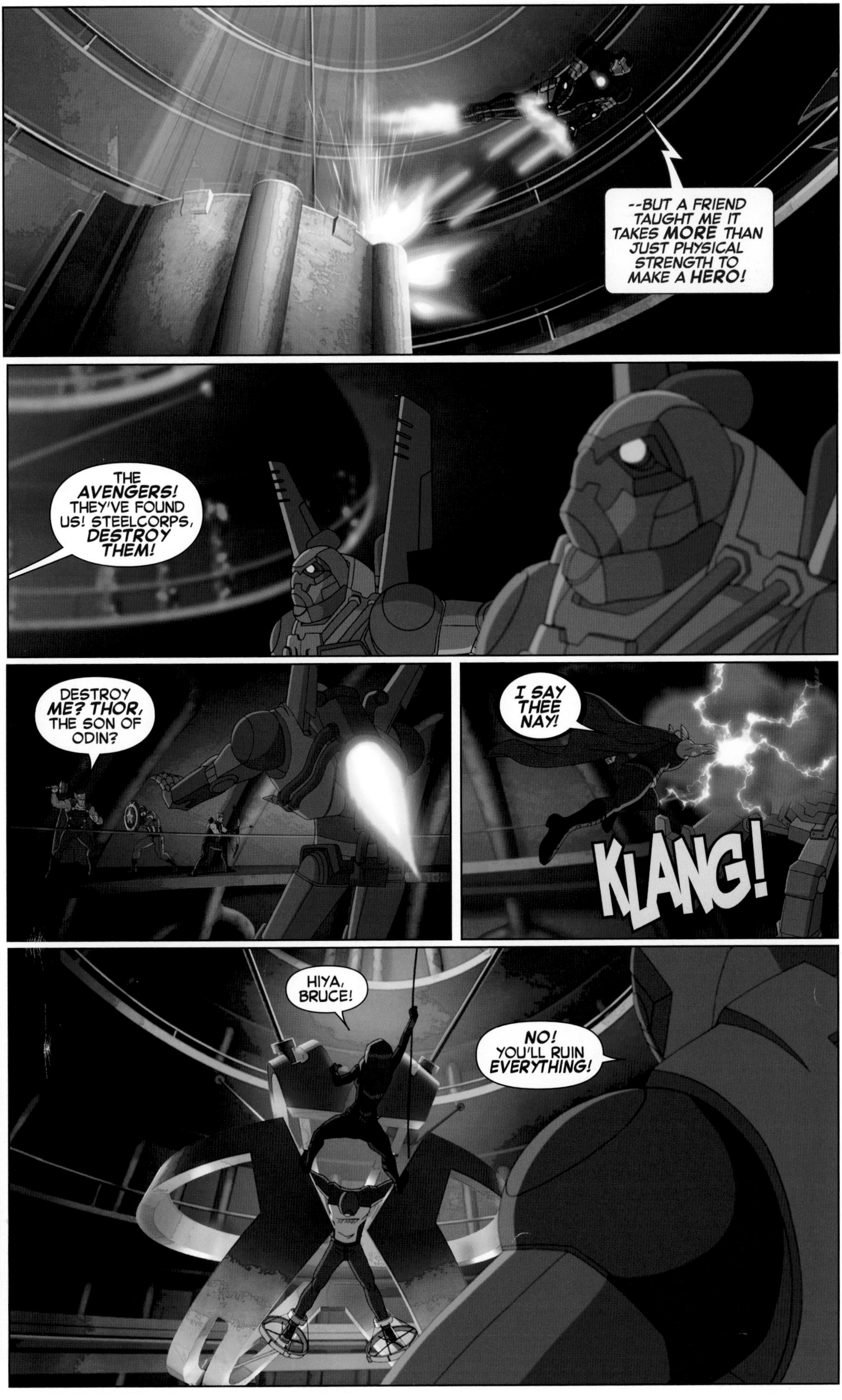
--BUT A FRIEND TAUGHT ME IT TAKES MORE THAN JUST PHYSICAL STRENGTH TO MAKE A HERO!
THE AVENGERS! THEY'VE FOUND US! STEELCORPS, DESTROY THEM!
DESTROY ME? THOR, THE SON OF ODIN?
I SAY THEE NAY!
KLANG!
HIYA, BRUCE!
NO! YOU'LL RUIN EVERYTHING!

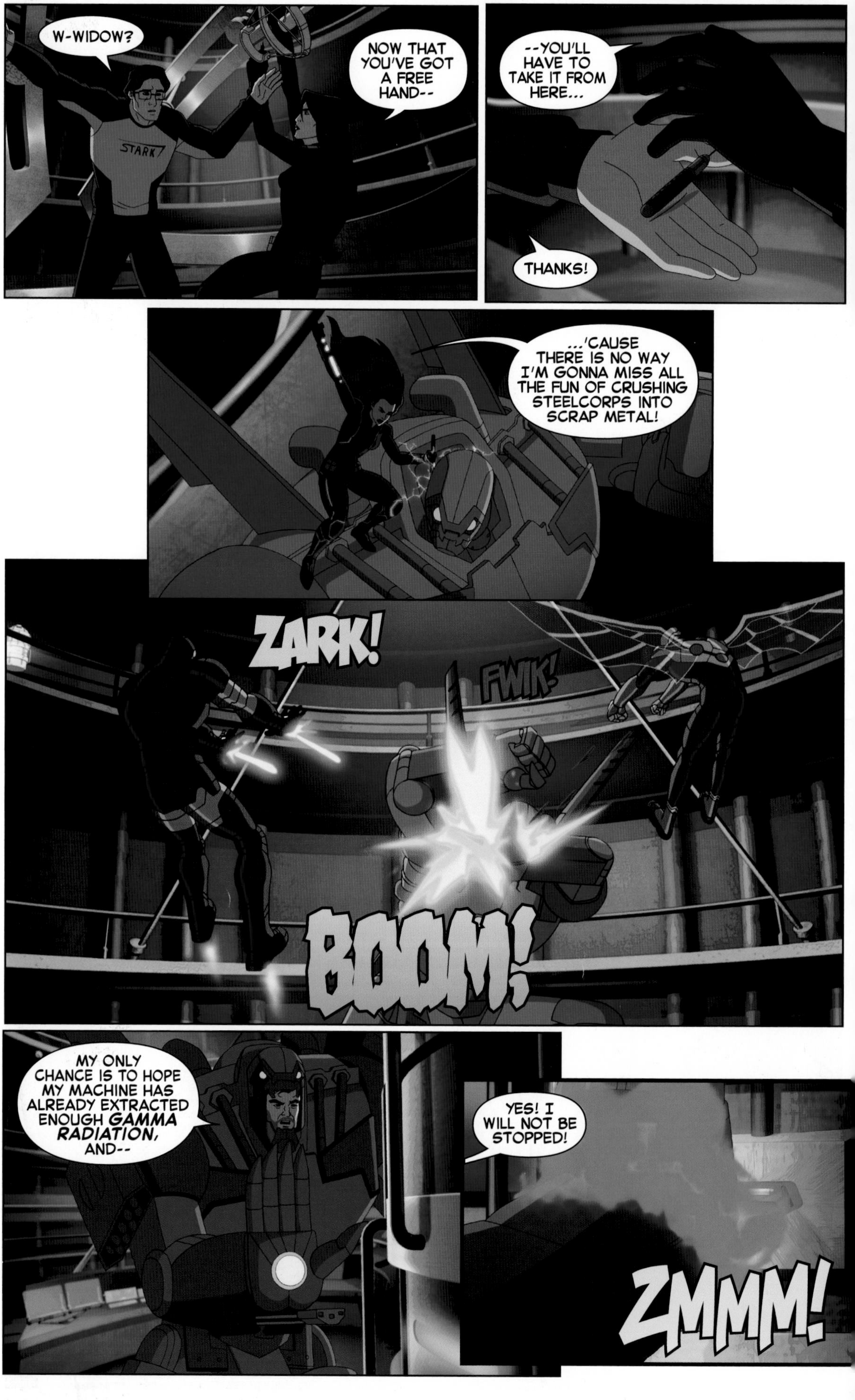
W-WIDOW?
NOW THAT YOU'VE GOT A FREE HAND--
--YOU'LL HAVE TO TAKE IT FROM HERE...
THANKS!
...'CAUSE THERE IS NO WAY I'M GONNA MISS ALL THE FUN OF CRUSHING STEELCORPS INTO SCRAP METAL!
ZARK!
FWIK!
BOOM!
MY ONLY CHANCE IS TO HOPE MY MACHINE HAS ALREADY EXTRACTED ENOUGH *GAMMA RADIATION*, AND--
YES! I WILL NOT BE STOPPED!
ZMMM!

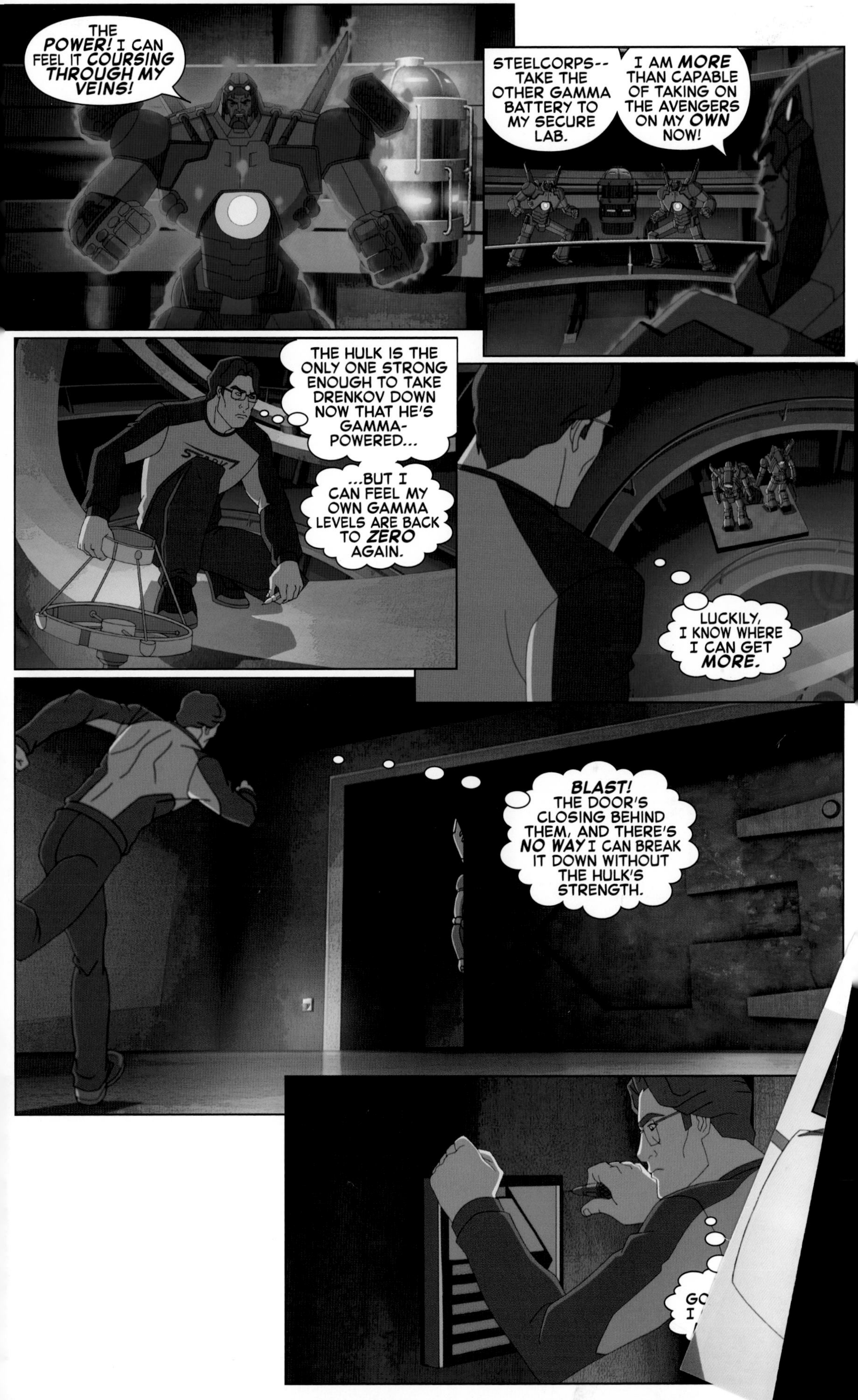
THE POWER! I CAN FEEL IT COURSING THROUGH MY VEINS!
STEELCORPS-- TAKE THE OTHER GAMMA BATTERY TO MY SECURE LAB.
I AM MORE THAN CAPABLE OF TAKING ON THE AVENGERS ON MY OWN NOW!
THE HULK IS THE ONLY ONE STRONG ENOUGH TO TAKE DRENKOV DOWN NOW THAT HE'S GAMMA-POWERED...
...BUT I CAN FEEL MY OWN GAMMA LEVELS ARE BACK TO ZERO AGAIN.
LUCKILY, I KNOW WHERE I CAN GET MORE.
BLAST! THE DOOR'S CLOSING BEHIND THEM, AND THERE'S NO WAY I CAN BREAK IT DOWN WITHOUT THE HULK'S STRENGTH.

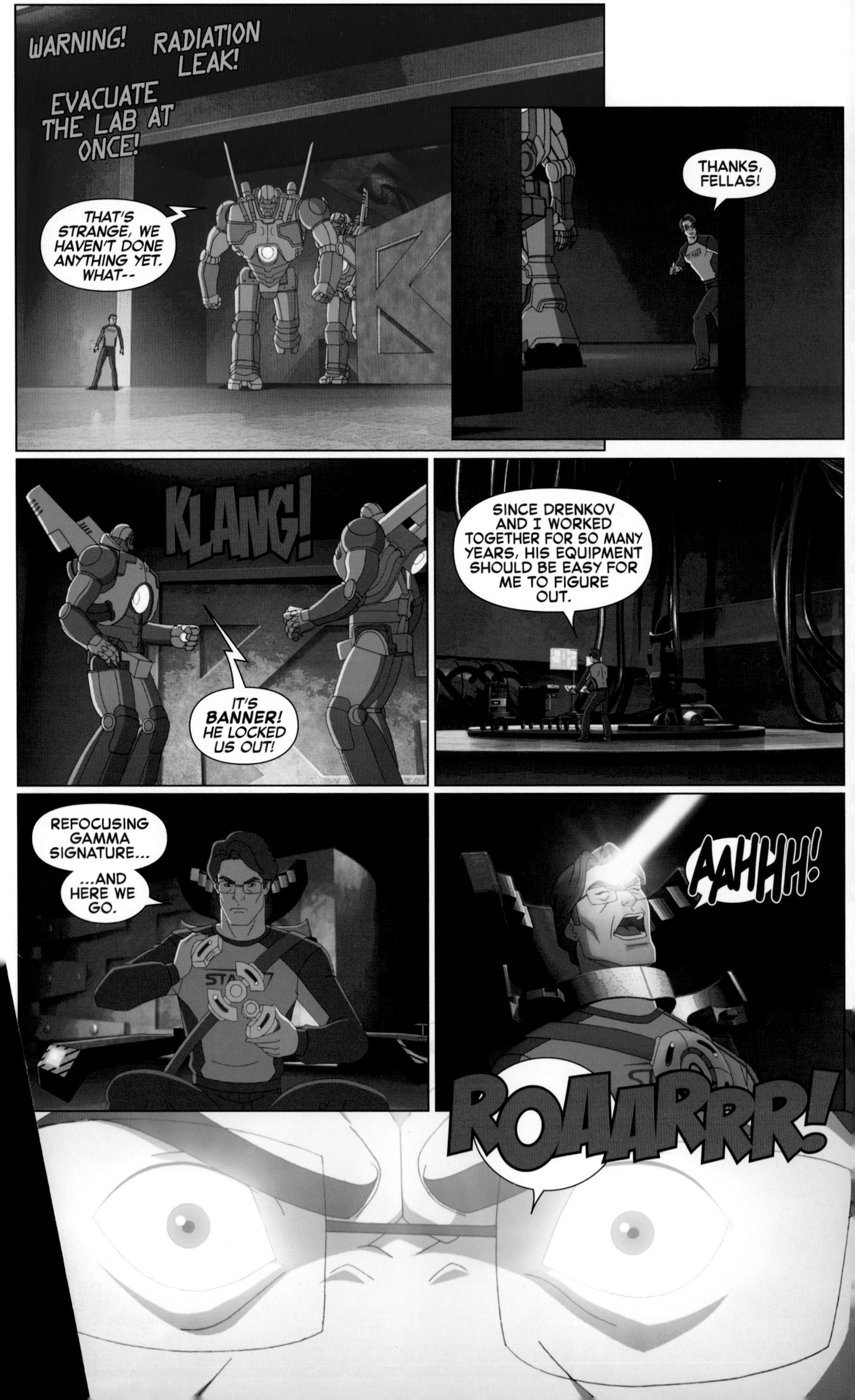

WARNING! RADIATION LEAK!
EVACUATE THE LAB AT ONCE!
THAT'S STRANGE, WE HAVEN'T DONE ANYTHING YET. WHAT--
THANKS, FELLAS!
KLANG!
IT'S BANNER! HE LOCKED US OUT!
SINCE DRENKOV AND I WORKED TOGETHER FOR SO MANY YEARS, HIS EQUIPMENT SHOULD BE EASY FOR ME TO FIGURE OUT.
REFOCUSING GAMMA SIGNATURE...
...AND HERE WE GO.
AAHHH!
ROAARRR!

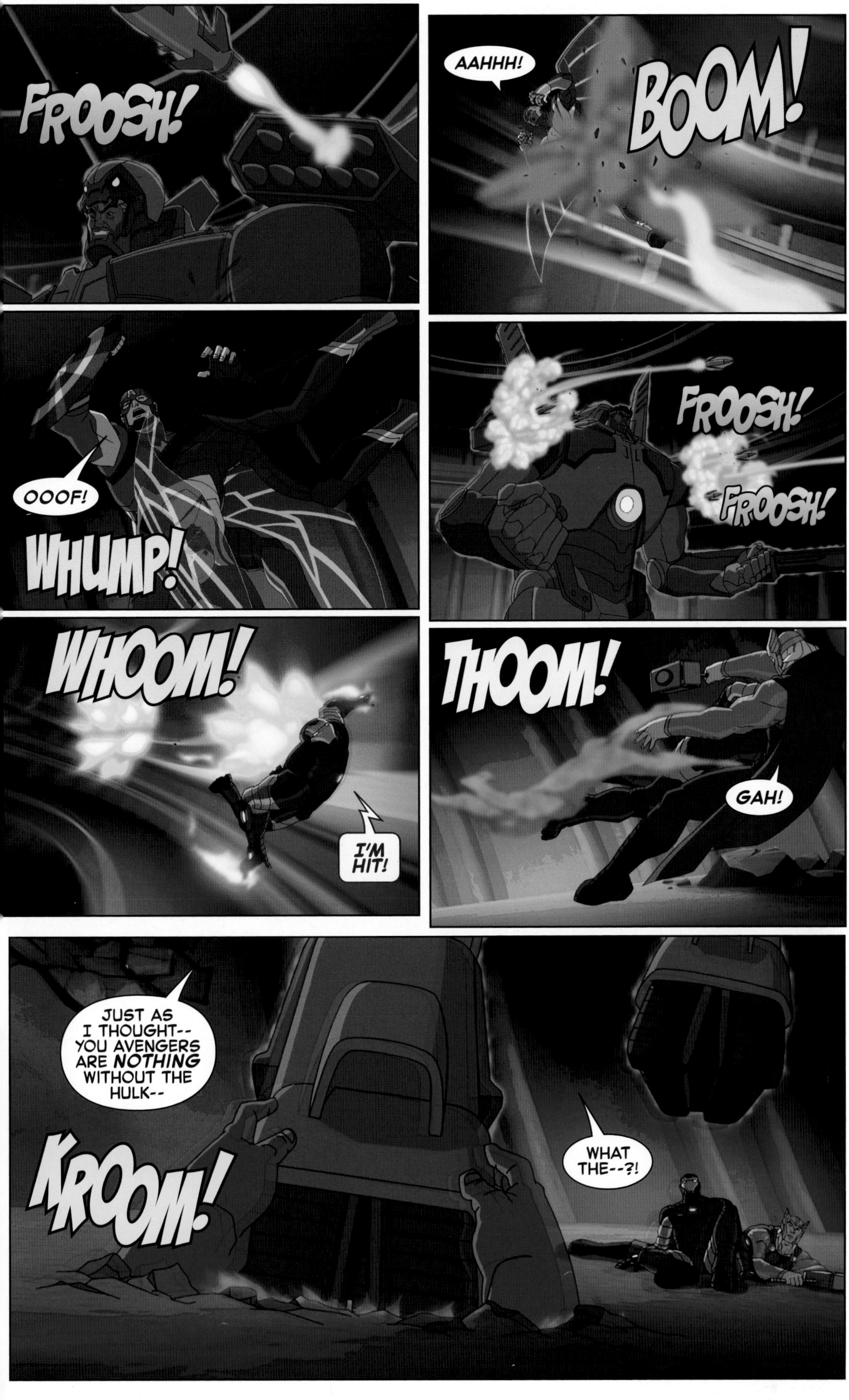
FROOSH!
AAHHH!
BOOM!
OOOF!
WHUMP!
FROOSH!
FROOSH!
WHOOM!
I'M HIT!
THOOM!
GAH!
JUST AS I THOUGHT-- YOU AVENGERS ARE NOTHING WITHOUT THE HULK--
KROOM!
WHAT THE--?!

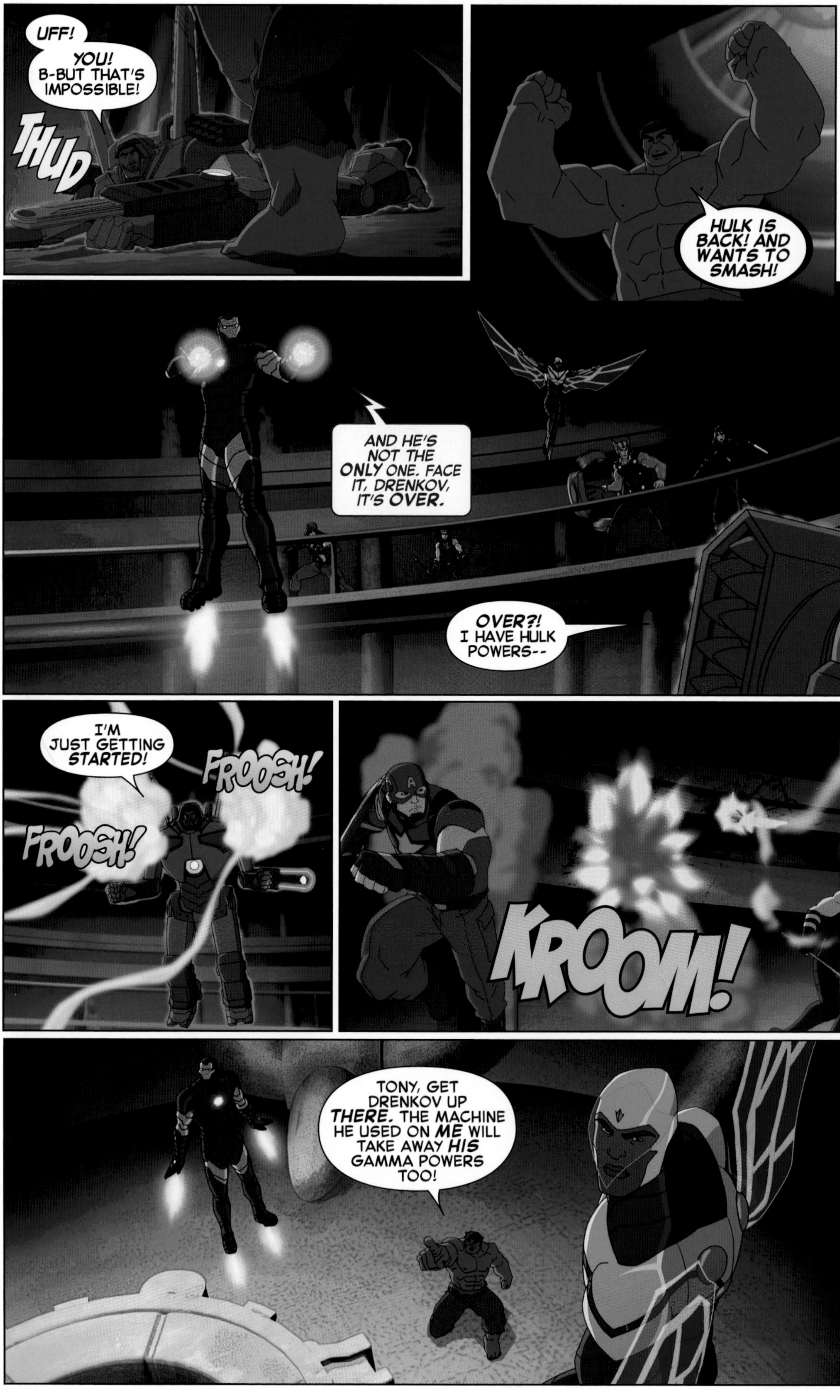
UFF!
YOU! B-BUT THAT'S IMPOSSIBLE!
THUD
HULK IS BACK! AND WANTS TO SMASH!
AND HE'S NOT THE ONLY ONE. FACE IT, DRENKOV, IT'S OVER.
OVER?! I HAVE HULK POWERS--
I'M JUST GETTING STARTED!
FROOSH!
FROOSH!
KROOOM!
TONY, GET DRENKOV UP THERE. THE MACHINE HE USED ON ME WILL TAKE AWAY HIS GAMMA POWERS TOO!

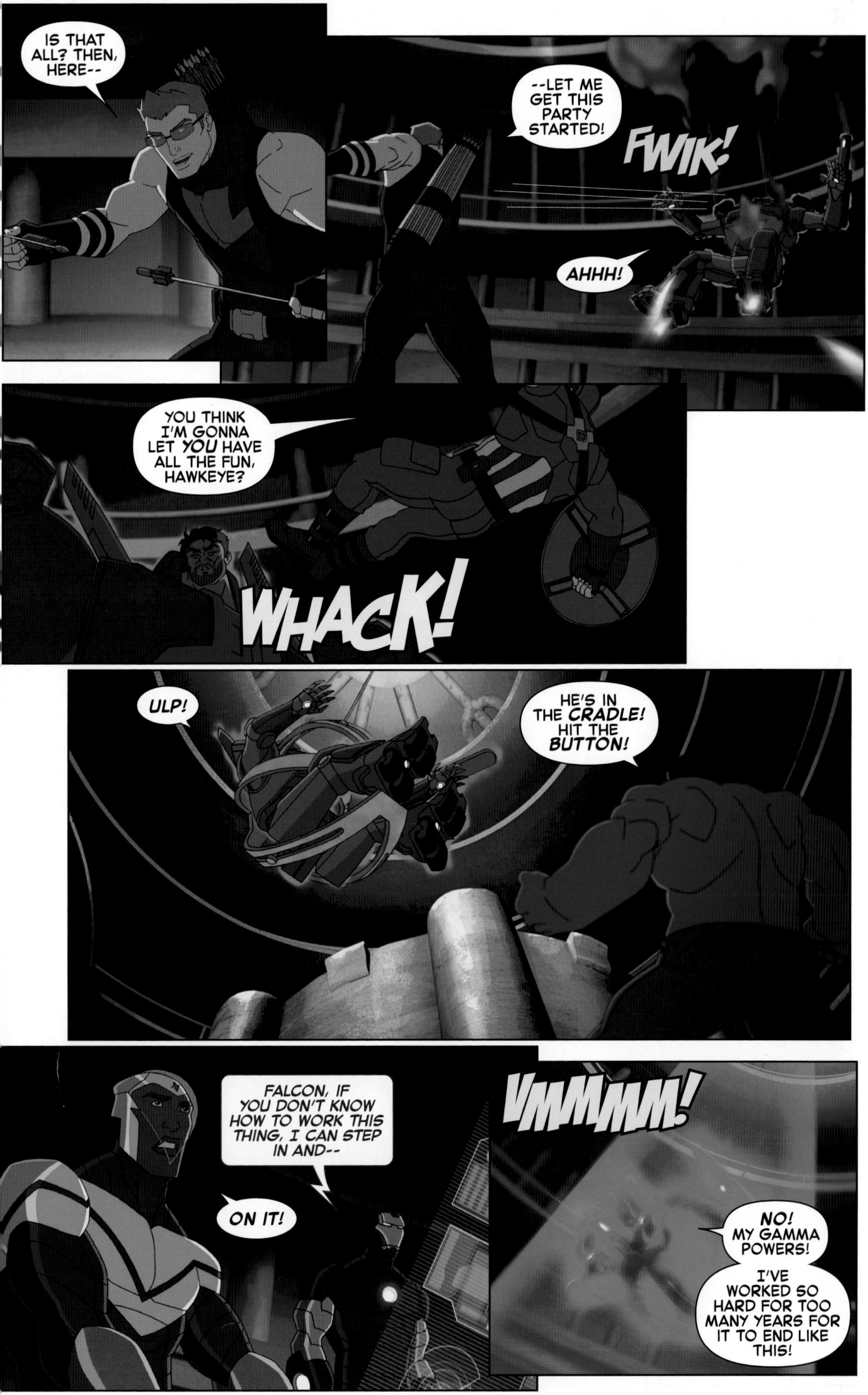
IS THAT ALL? THEN, HERE--
--LET ME GET THIS PARTY STARTED!
FWIK!
AHHH!
YOU THINK I'M GONNA LET YOU HAVE ALL THE FUN, HAWKEYE?
WHACK!
ULP!
HE'S IN THE CRADLE! HIT THE BUTTON!
FALCON, IF YOU DON'T KNOW HOW TO WORK THIS THING, I CAN STEP IN AND--
ON IT!
VMMMMM!
NO! MY GAMMA POWERS!
I'VE WORKED SO HARD FOR TOO MANY YEARS FOR IT TO END LIKE THIS!

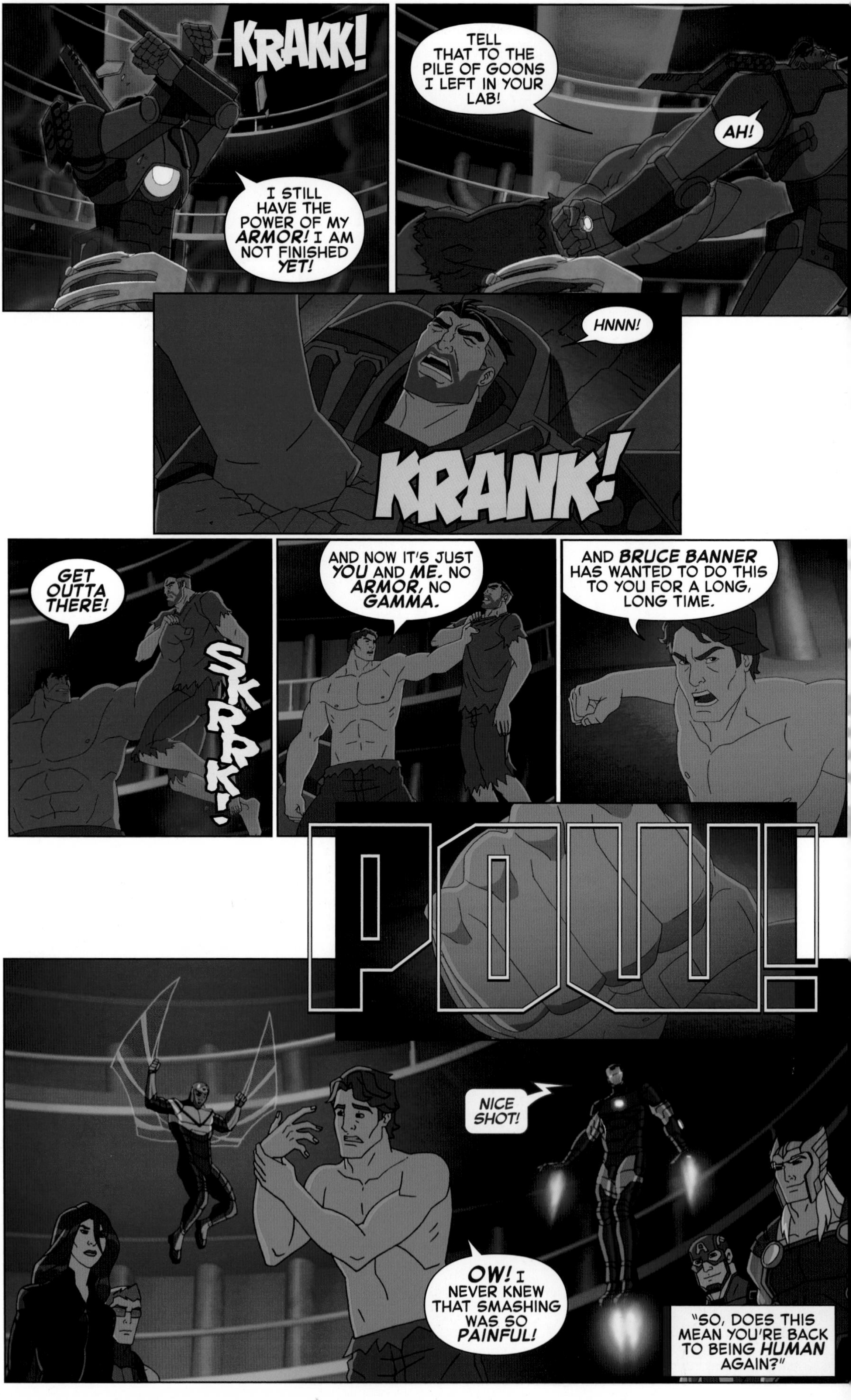
KRAKK!
I STILL HAVE THE POWER OF MY ARMOR! I AM NOT FINISHED YET!
TELL THAT TO THE PILE OF GOONS I LEFT IN YOUR LAB!
AH!
HNNN!
KRANK!
GET OUTTA THERE!
SKRRK!
AND NOW IT'S JUST YOU AND ME. NO ARMOR, NO GAMMA.
AND BRUCE BANNER HAS WANTED TO DO THIS TO YOU FOR A LONG, LONG TIME.
POW!
NICE SHOT!
OW! I NEVER KNEW THAT SMASHING WAS SO PAINFUL!
"SO, DOES THIS MEAN YOU'RE BACK TO BEING HUMAN AGAIN?"

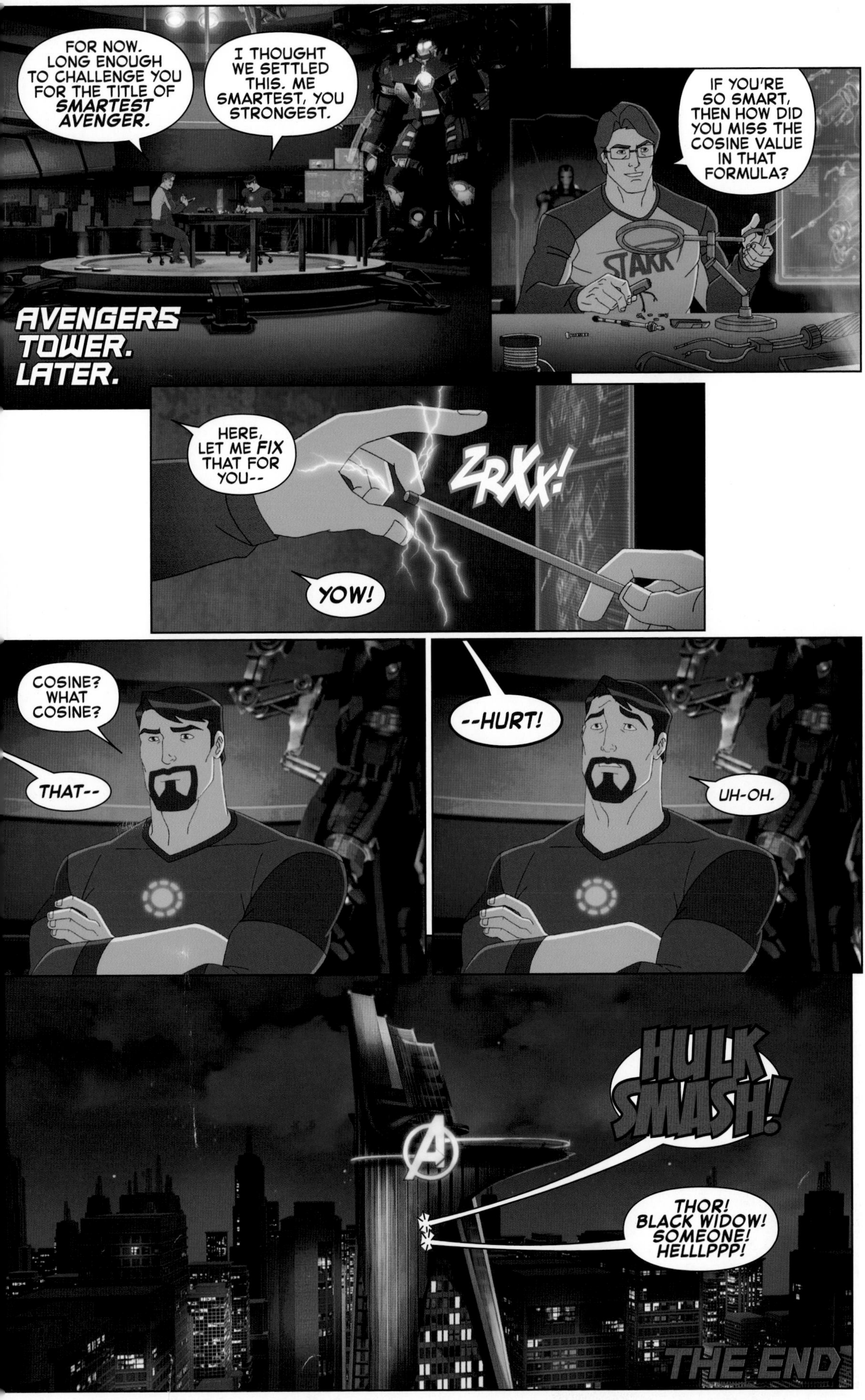
FOR NOW. LONG ENOUGH TO CHALLENGE YOU FOR THE TITLE OF SMARTEST AVENGER.
I THOUGHT WE SETTLED THIS. ME SMARTEST, YOU STRONGEST.
AVENGERS TOWER. LATER.
IF YOU'RE SO SMART, THEN HOW DID YOU MISS THE COSINE VALUE IN THAT FORMULA?
STARK
HERE, LET ME FIX THAT FOR YOU--
ZRKX!
YOW!
COSINE? WHAT COSINE?
THAT--
--HURT!
UH-OH.
HULK SMASH!
THOR! BLACK WIDOW! SOMEONE! HELLLPPP!
THE END

MARVEL

AVENGERS ULTRON REVOLUTION®

COLLECT THEM ALL!

Set of 4 Hardcover Books ISBN: 978-1-5321-4345-8

MARVEL
AVENGERS
ULTRON REVOLUTION
ADAPTING TO CHANGE #1

Hardcover Book ISBN
978-1-5321-4346-5

MARVEL
AVENGERS
ULTRON REVOLUTION
THE ULTIMATES #2

Hardcover Book ISBN
978-1-5321-4347-2

MARVEL
AVENGERS
ULTRON REVOLUTION
SAVING CAPTAIN ROGERS #3

Hardcover Book ISBN
978-1-5321-4348-9

MARVEL
AVENGERS
ULTRON REVOLUTION
DEHULKED #4

Hardcover Book ISBN
978-1-5321-4349-6